Luck and Love

A Lucky In Love Novella (A Second Chance Contemporary Romance)

Bestselling & International Bestselling Author

April Lynn Baker

Copyright © 2022 by April Lynn Baker

All rights reserved. The material in this book is copyrighted and licensed for your personal enjoyment only. It may not be re-sold or given away to other people. If you would like to share this book with another person, please purchase an additional copy for each recipient. If you are reading this book and did not purchase it or it was not purchased for your use only, then please delete and purchase your own copy.

This is a work of fiction. Any names, places, characters, and incidents either are the product of the author's imagination or are used fictitiously. Any resemblance to any actual persons, living or dead, organizations, events or locales are entirely coincidental.

No part of this book may be reproduced, stored in a retrieval system, or transmitted by any means without the written permission of the author.

Thank you for respecting the hard work of the author.

Cover by MK Moore

Editing by Rainlyt Editing

Formatting by MK Moore

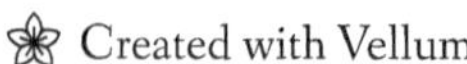 Created with Vellum

Disclaimer

All care has been taken to make sure the names are fictional and any similarities to living or dead is purely coincidental. No group/club (etc.) is affiliated in any way to this work.
Warning:
This book contains situations that are not suitable to anyone under 18 due to sexual scenes.

LUCKY IN LOVE

LUCK AND LOVE

Bestselling Author

April Lynn Baker

Blurb

Shane

Tiffany was once mine, until I made the wrong decision to leave town for the military.
Now I'm back and seeing her again has brought back old feelings.
Will she give me a second chance or has my luck run out?

Chapter One
Shane

I just got back into town from the airport. The town I'm from hasn't changed much. I left Spring Meadows five years ago to join the military. Now I'm heading to my brother's bar to get the keys to his house. I'll be staying there until I find my own place. It's almost St. Patrick's Day and the bar will more than likely be packed until after. I left behind a lot of people, including the one person I regret ever leaving: Tiffany, my ex-girlfriend. She didn't exactly agree with my career choice. She said she couldn't deal with it if I didn't come home.

The taxi pulls up to the bar and I get out, heading inside. I have to shove my way through crowd just to get to the hallway that will lead me to my brother's office.

"Did you miss me, jackass?" I say, and my brother lifts his head from the papers he's looking over and smiles at me. We are twins, and I have missed him a lot.

"Good to have you back, asshole," he says and points to the chairs in front of his desk. I take a seat and place all my belongings in the chair next to me.

"It's good to have you home, man."

"Same here. It's been a long time but I see the town hasn't changed much."

"A few places moved in, bringing more tourists to the town."

"Max, how's Tiff been?" I ask and he sighs, running his hands through his hair.

"She's getting by. She's working at the diner. But there's something you need to know."

"What do you mean?"

"I think it's best that you go see her."

"She wants nothing to do with me. She's the one who left."

"Actually, you left her."

"You know I couldn't stay."

"I know, man, but she was broken when you left."

I couldn't stay because my father had passed away right before and I couldn't deal with the pain. He was my role model growing up and he's the reason I joined the Army.

"I'll stop by sometime and see her. Right now, I need rest."

"The key is above the door. Stay as long as you need to," he says, and I nod before leaving his office. I'm kind of scared to see Tiffany after this long because we didn't end on good terms. I left her crying on the sidewalk outside of the airport and never looked back.

Chapter Two
Tiffany

I'm fifteen minutes late to work because my son, Luke, decided he wanted to wait for his father to come into town. Not once did I keep who his dad was from him. I just wasn't ready to see him. I dropped Luke off at school and now I'm walking into the diner for my shift. I am a waitress and make good money doing it.

I haven't been with anyone since Shane and never will be. I still love him even though he decided to leave. I couldn't understand why at the time, and wish I could take it back. He needed my support and I didn't give it to him.

"Mike was by here already looking for you," Michelle, the owner, tells me as I am putting on my apron and getting ready to take orders. Mike is the sheriff and has been trying to get together with me, but I don't want to. It's bordering on harassment and stalking.

"I wish he would just give up. I'm not interested."

"I hear Shane is back," she says, smiling.

"Yes, he is, but I'm not ready."

I take my pad in hand and head over to my first table. The person at it is Shane himself. I steel my nerves and pray to God that I don't act like a fool. His head is shaved but not completely bald and he's wearing his uniform. My heart is beating a little too fast and I can't control my breathing. He has always had my heart and soul and always will.

"What can I get you?" I stutter. I take a calming breath.

He looks up at me, his chocolate brown eyes meeting mine. "Good to see you again, Tiff," he says and smiles. Damn it! I have never been able to resist him and his devilish smile.

"Same here," I whisper.

"Give me a coffee, black, and an order of biscuits and gravy."

"I'll be right back with your coffee," I say, and stride away from his table. He's probably watching my ass as I walk away. It's one of the things he has always loved about my body.

"I see Shane is here," Michelle says as I walk up to the window of the kitchen and place the order down on the edge so Harry can get it.

"Was he here the whole time?"

"He actually arrived before you did."

"Why didn't you tell me?"

"Because you two need to make up."

She's right, I do need to make things right. But I don't know how to go about telling him about Luke. I knew I was pregnant when he left town and I didn't tell him. Maybe if I had he would have stayed. I'll give myself a couple days and then talk to him, because I need to brace myself for his reaction. Hopefully it doesn't cause a bigger wedge between us.

Chapter Three
Shane

I just left the restaurant and am now heading to my brother's house. I wanted to talk to Tiffany but her job isn't the place. Michelle handed me a piece of paper as I was leaving and told me go see her. I plan on doing that after I get some rest. I walk into the house and see that my brother is here, so I head into his spare room and set my stuff down before joining him in the living room.

"What are you doing home already?" I ask, taking a seat on the chair next to the couch. He hands me a beer and I open it, taking a swig.

"Finished up my paperwork early. Nothing else to do."

"I went by the diner and saw Tiff. She's gained some weight, man. I freaking love it."

"Did you talk to her?"

"Not much. She was busy working. I'm going by her house when she gets off work."

"She actually gave you her address?"

"Nope. Michelle did."

"Hopefully you get shit straightened out."

"I plan on it."

I want my woman back and I will do anything to make that happen. Seeing her after all these years makes me yearn to feel her body next to mine. Sex wasn't ever an issue in our relationship. Different career paths was, and now that I'm out, I plan on making up for lost time.

Chapter Four
Tiffany

I just got home from picking Luke up from school. He had a good day but is upset that I'm not letting him see his father. I want him to, but it's not the right time. I need to come to terms that he's actually back. I hear a knock in the door and Luke gets up to answer it.

"If it's the sheriff, tell him to come back later," I say as I stop next to Luke at the door. But it isn't Mike that's standing there, it's Shane. He's dressed in blue jeans, a black t-shirt, and a blue jean jacket. It's cold out, but not too cold.

"Shane!"

"May I come in or are you going to make me stand out here?" he says and we move out of the way so he can enter the house. How did he know where I lived?

"What are you doing here?" I ask him as he takes a seat on the couch.

"We need to talk."

"Luke, why don't you go play in your room for a while?" I tell him, and he heads down the hallway to his room.

"Talk about what, Shane?"

"Who's his father?" Shane asks, and I look down at the table in front of me. I know at some point I would have told him about Luke, but I didn't think it would be now.

"You."

"He looks just like me when I was that age."

"He acts just like you too," I say and give him a small smile.

"This is why my brother told me to talk to you, isn't it?"

"He has been helping when he can. After you left, he stepped in to make sure his nephew didn't want for anything. I wanted to tell you before you left, but I got scared," I say, and tears well up in my eyes.

"I'm sorry I left the way I did," he says and stands up, heading towards me. He takes my face in his hands and I look up into his big brown eyes.

"I lost a part of me when you did," I say, tears running down my face. He takes one of his fingers and wipes away some of the tears.

"I missed you, Tiff, and not a day went by that I wasn't thinking of you."

"You were my one and only and always will be. I've not been with anyone but you."

"Why? I never expected you to wait on me."

"You were my first and my heart belongs to you."

"I want us to be a family, Tiff, and I will wait for however long it takes. I didn't leave to get away from you. I left to get away from the pain. Please believe that," he says, tears in his eyes.

"I want the same but I'm not ready yet."

"I'll give you all the time you need, but I do want to officially meet my son."

"Mommy, is everything okay?" Luke asks as he walks into the living room.

"Yes, I'm fine, baby," I say as I wipe my face with my hands. "Luke, this is your daddy. Want to come say hi?"

Luke walks over and stands in front of Shane, looking up at him. He's been waiting for this day and so have I. I never hid his dad from him because his dad isn't a bad man; he just got lost when his father died.

"Hi, I'm Luke. Mommy is always telling me how I look like you."

"You do. She wasn't lying about that," Shane says, kneeling down in front of him. Luke catapults himself into Shane's arms and wraps his arms around his waist, holding on for dear life.

"Are you and Mommy getting back together?" he asks, looking up at his dad.

"That's up to Mommy. Right now we are talking things out."

"I hope you do. I don't like seeing Mommy sad all the time," he says, and sobs break free.

I didn't think he even noticed. I try to hide it because I don't want him worrying. He's a kid and deserves to be happy and carefree.

"I never stopped loving your mom. We just need to work things out. Got it, buddy?"

Luke nods and buries himself into Shane's body. This has been a long time coming and I'm glad that he took the initiative to talk to Shane. I thought he would be all shy, but not my son. He has his dad's personality and that isn't a bad thing.

Chapter Five
Shane

All I can do is look down at the small boy that I helped create. He fell asleep not long ago in my lap and I don't want to move him just yet. I can't believe that I have an almost five-year-old son.

"He's perfect, Tiff," I say and look over at her. She's sitting on the couch, covered up in a blanket. The smile she has on her face and the look in her eyes tell me that she's happy and content. Her smile is why I fell in love with her, and her personality is why I love her. I wasn't lying to my son when I said that I never stopped loving her.

"Shane, what are we doing?" she asks, and I look back down at Luke. What I wouldn't give to have his little feet running around in our house. But I don't want to rush things.

"Getting to know each other again."

"You going to take me on dates!" she says, smiling.

"If you want me to," I say, smiling back.

"Yes. We have a party at the bar downtown every St. Patrick's Day. Want to go?"

"Sure, I'll pick you up at 6pm. Right now I have to get back to that same bar, so I can start my job," I say and carefully remove Luke from my lap. I lay him on the couch and head towards the woman I love, bending down and kissing her on the head.

"I'll see you in a couple of days."

"You sure will," she says, and I head out. Two days and I'll hopefully have her in my bed, begging me for more and screaming out my name. This is the first step to claiming what has always been mine and having my son in my life fulltime.

Chapter Six
Tiffany

I am sitting here at the counter in the diner, thinking about Shane. I haven't been able to get him off my mind since yesterday and it's driving me crazy. All the memories and feelings are coming back and I don't know how to deal with them.

"You okay?" I hear Michelle ask, and I look up from the counter I have been staring at for the last twenty minutes.

"Yeah. Just thinking about stuff."

"Does this happen to be about a sexy ex-soldier?" she asks, a smirk on her face. Michelle is like a mother to me. She stepped in to help steer me in the right direction when my mother passed away, about a year after Shane had left.

"Yes! I can't stop thinking about him. I kind of asked him to be my date tomorrow."

"Well, that's a good thing. You two have always been perfect together."

"Yes, we were. I just wish I had dealt with it better when he left."

"You were hurt and scared."

"I was more scared that I would never see him again."

"Well, he's back and you should leap and get your love back."

"I plan on it," I say, smiling like the fool I am.

What happens if we get back together, only for him to end things again? I can't have him in and out of our lives, especially since he and Luke met and spent time together. I don't want to see how broken he would be. I need to make sure that doesn't happen again.

Chapter Seven
Shane

I can't stop thinking about Tiff, no matter how hard I try. She was what got me through tough times overseas. The thought of coming back and being with her again is what kept me sane. I am currently at my brother's bar because today I start my new job as his bouncer. The other one just up and quit for no reason.

"Just make sure you don't hurt them too much. I would hate for you to end up in jail," I hear my brother say and I nod. I wouldn't hurt anyone, unless they swing first.

"Got it."

"How's Tiff?"

"She's good. I met Luke yesterday. Why didn't you tell me?"

"Wasn't my place."

"Anyways, thank you for what you've done for them. I just wish it was me taking care of them."

"I understand why you left, man, and you're welcome. I am his uncle."

My brother and I have always had a close relationship, but when my father died, I shut everyone out. The pain was just too much and I couldn't stay. Sometime, I need to go see my mom and let her know

I'm back. She suffered just as much as I did and I completely stopped talking to her.

"How's mom?" I say, and he looks down at the beer bottle in his hands, then back at me.

"She was a mess when you left. She went through a bought of depression, but she pulled through. Luke is what kept her sane all these years. She misses you, bro, and I think you need to go see her."

"I'll go see her tomorrow before I go pick up Tiff for the party."

"You two back together?"

"No. Just taking things slow. But eventually we will be."

"There is no slow with you. You and Tiff have always clashed together."

"That's true, man, but I want things to go right this time. This is my second chance and I'm not about to mess it up."

"I hear ya."

I've got a lot of work ahead of me to get Tiffany to trust me again. Never in a million years did I ever think I would be a father, and it scares the shit out of me. One thing I know is that my son will never think that I don't love and care for him. That's one thing my dad taught me: to take care of my own and never let go.

Chapter Eight
Tiffany

I already miss Shane, and Luke has already been asking when he's going to see his dad again. I keep telling him that his dad has started a new job and is really busy right now. In all reality, I can pick up the phone and message him, but I'm still scared. I want this time to work out right, for the sake of our son. I need to know that he's fully invested in us.

"Mommy, Daddy is here!" my son yells in excitement, and I come around the corner from the kitchen. Shane is standing there with some roses in his hands and a smile on his handsome face.

"I was wondering if you wanted to come with me to see my mom," he says, and Luke breaks out in a happy dance. He loves going to see her because he's the only grandchild and he gets spoiled.

"Sure, let me put these in water and get ready," I say, taking the roses from his hands and heading into the kitchen. Shane knows roses have always been my weakness. Every day he was giving me roses, and at one point my room at my mom's house looked like an actual flower shop.

"Okay. Let's get going. I have to be at the bar later to help set up for the party tomorrow," I say, and Shane grabs my hand in his. As soon as my skin touches his, I feel the all-too-familiar electricity going up my arm. We've always had a deep connection.

"I'll have you there by five. My brother told me what time you have to be there," he says and winks.

What I wouldn't give to have his plump and kissable lips on mine, his hands exploring my body and his tongue torturing my pussy. He has always known my body better than me.

"Let's get going," I say, clearing my throat.

"I'm going to mamaw's!" Luke yells out and is out the door before anyone can stop him. We follow him out and I lock the door behind me. He leads us over to his truck and helps us get in. Once we are settled, he starts it up and we pull off.

Twenty minutes later, we are pulling up in front of her house. Luke is getting restless in the back seat. Shane gets him out and then Luke's running up the pathway and knocking on the door.

"He really loves your mom."

"I can see that," he says and smiles.

He takes ahold of my hand again and we head up the pathway. The door swings open, his mom Ethel standing there. She notices Shane and a wide smile forms on her face, tears in her eyes.

"Shane! I didn't know you were back," she says and takes her son into her arms, hugging him.

"I told Max not to tell you. I wanted it to be a surprise," Shane says, his voice thick with emotion.

"I see that you now know you're a father."

"Yes. I've missed so much with him. But plan to be here for everything else."

"Tiffany, it's good to see that beautiful smile on your face again," Ethel says and hugs me.

"I am happy, but taking things slow," I say and Ethel leads us into the house. Nothing has changed a bit in the house. It's cozy as always.

"Take a seat and I'll get some drinks and snacks," Ethel says and heads into the kitchen, Luke on her heels.

"This place hasn't changed," I hear Shane say, and I give him a small smile. He hasn't been back here since his dad died.

"Your mom didn't want to get rid of anything."

"I'm glad she didn't. So many memories."

I step up to him and take his hand in mine, letting him know that I'm here for support. His dad was a good man and he was gone too soon. Everything in this house is a reminder of that. His dad built this house from the ground up, so his family would have a place to live and grow up. All the money he had at the time went into this house. After that, he worked two jobs until he was back on his feet.

"You are just like your father, son," his mom says, coming back in from the kitchen.

"How so, mom?" he asks.

"Your father did everything in his power to make sure that we were happy and taken care of. Family was always first in his eyes. Our love never wavered and never burnt out. It was strong till the day he died and will forever endure."

"But I left my family," he says, confusion marring his face.

"Fate knew you weren't ready at the time, but it gave Tiffany a gift that helped her when she needed it most. Now, fate has brought you three together and I think it's time that you two have what your father and I had," his mom says, tears running down her face.

She's right; neither one of us was ready at the time. I had Luke and he's what kept me happy. Shane was off protecting people and becoming the man who is standing in front of me. Strong, caring, loving, and dependable. I wouldn't change anything that happened all those years ago, because we have our second chance.

Chapter Nine
Shane

We left my mom's house and are just now pulling up to the bar so I can drop Tiffany off. I told her I would keep Luke so he's not in the way. Plus, he's already asleep and I don't want to wake him yet. My mom said a lot of things that have me thinking. She's right; I wasn't ready.

"I'll be here to pick you up at seven," I tell her and she nods, getting out of the truck. She's been lost in her head since the conversation at my mom's. I pull out of the bar parking lot and head towards my brother's. I plan on having a fun evening with my son.

"Come on, buddy," I say and lift him into my arms, carrying him inside. I lay him on the couch, then head into the kitchen to find something for dinner.

"Can we have pizza?" he asks, walking into the kitchen. He's rubbing his eyes and smiling up at me. He has my brown hair, brown eyes, and smile.

"Sure, keeps me from cooking and burning the house down," I say and pull out my phone, dialing the number. When I've ordered our food, we head into the living room.

"Pick out a movie to watch," I tell him, and he heads over to the

DVD tower, looking through them. When he's picked one, he runs back over to me.

"Are you sure about this one?" I ask and look down at him

"Yes, I watch it all the time. I love the fighting," he says and climbs up on the couch next to me.

"Okay. As long as your mom won't mind," I say and put the DVD in, then push play. It shouldn't be long before our food gets here. I sit back and Luke cuddles into my body.

"How's school going, little man?"

"Good. I like my teacher and I have lots of friends."

"You in kindergarten yet?"

"No. I don't turn five until a couple months, so Mommy says next year."

"Cool. I remember my kindergarten year. I didn't want to leave my mom. Threw a big fit."

"Really?" he asks and looks up at me.

"Yes. I was afraid that no one would like me. Turns out I made a lot of friends."

"Cool!" he says and turns his attention back to the movie. He picked out Mortal Kombat, which is my favorite movie. There is a knock at the door and I get up to answer it. It's the pizza guy, so I pay him and carry the food into the living room and set it on the coffee table.

"Time to eat, bud. Then we have to head back out to get Mommy," I say, and we dig in. He told me that pepperoni was his favorite, so that's what I got.

"How about tomorrow before we drop you off at mamaw's, we go to get ice cream or something?"

"Can I get a toy?" he asks, his face lighting up.

"Sure, we can do that," I tell him and ruffle his hair. He is so much like me when I was his age.

"Okay, let's go get Mommy," I say once we've finished eating, and we exit the house. I put him in the truck, then buckle him in. Time to go get Tiffany and get them home so my son can get some rest.

Chapter Ten
Tiffany

"Follow me. I'll show you to his room so you can lay him down," I tell Shane, and he follows me down the hallway. He lays him in his bed and takes off his coat and shoes, covering him up.

"He's had a full day. Hopefully he'll sleep all night," he tells me, before planting a kiss on his head.

"Thank you for keeping him."

"It's not a problem. He's my son so I want to be in his life."

"I was thinking about what your mom said today. I don't want to lose another chance at being with you. You are it for me, Shane," I confess, then wait for him to reply.

"What are you saying, Tiff?"

"I want us to be together, a family."

"I thought you wanted to take it slow?"

"I see you with him and it makes me happy. He's already grown attached to you and I don't want to push you away anymore."

"I want the same, but only if you are sure," he says and grabs me, pulling me into his body and wrapping me up in his strong, familiar arms.

"I love you, Shane, and I'm sure," I say, and he leans down, his lips touching mine. I open my mouth, allowing him access, and his tongue clashes with mine. I moan and he grabs ahold of my ass and squeezes. This is how I remember us being, the sparks when we kiss and the electricity when our bodies touch. He ends the kiss and looks down at me, lust shining in his brown eyes.

"I love you and always have, Tiff. I promise this time I'm not screwing this up."

"I believe you, Shane."

And I do believe him. He's not once lied about anything since we met and got together in high school. His attention has always been on me. He was the dark and badass to my light and innocent. He was my first and will be my last.

Chapter Eleven
Shane

It's the night of the St. Patrick's Day party at the bar and I'm guarding the door and making sure nothing bad happens. Everyone is dressed in green, guys clad in Leprechaun outfits and females in barely-there green dresses. Most have been drinking since the party started and are now drunk or getting there.

"Where's Tiff at?" my brother asks.

"She's in the bathroom changing. She wanted to surprise me with he outfit."

"Dude, you're falling and hard."

"She's always been mine."

"Tell that to the sheriff that won't take 'no' for an answer," my brother says, slurring his words. He's fucking drunk already.

"He touches her and I'll end him!" I growl, looking around for the woman I love.

She comes waking out of the hallway in the back. She's wearing a sparkling green dress with spaghetti straps. A v neckline comes down between her plump breasts and it molds perfectly to all her curves. My dick is pressing against my zipper painfully.

"Dude!" I hear Max say, and I look over at him.

"Quit eye fucking my woman!"

"Sorry, man, but damn. You have your hands full with that one."

"I fucking love her, bro."

"Then after your shift, take her."

"I plan on it," I say, and my beautiful woman strides up to me

"Like what you see?" she purrs, and I growl. She's a fucking temptress and she is loving every minute of making me squirm.

"You'll see later how much I love that dress on you!"

"I'm going to go mingle with your brother and Sophia. Come get me when you're free," she says, then sashays away. Her hips swaying and her plump ass jiggling has my dick getting harder. I see the sheriff start heading her way, so I start making my way through the crowd towards them.

"Mike, I have already told you I'm not interested," I hear Tiffany say as I walk up to them. He reaches out and grabs her by the waist, pulling her into his body. Hell, no! This fucker just fucked up.

"You know you want it. Look at how you're dressed," he slurs.

"Get off of me!" Tiff screams.

That's my cue to fuck the dude up. No one messes with what's mine. I grab the back of his shirt and pull him away from her. "She said no. Now leave or I'll throw you out!" I yell, and Tiff moves behind me, out of the way.

"Who the fuck are you?" he says, swaying back and forth. He looks like he's about to pass out. Some sheriff we've got here.

"She's taken, and you need to either chill or leave."

"So you are who she's whoring around with," he says, and I hear Tiff gasp behind me. That's it! I grab him by the shirt again and he swings on me. His fist hits me in jaw and two seconds later, I have him on the ground, face down, so he can't hit me again.

"I'm giving you one last chance to leave!" I growl.

He nods his head and I remove myself from his body, allowing him to get up. He looks over at Tiff and I move myself in front of her. He turns around and staggers through the crowd, then exits the bar.

"You okay?" I ask as I turn around to face her. She nods, and I take her into my arms, just holding her.

"Thank you," she murmurs into my chest, and I tighten my arms around her.

"You're welcome. It's my job to protect you."

"Are you off duty yet?" she asks, looking up at me.

"Another hour and I will be," I say.

"Want to get out of here after?"

"What do you have in mind?"

"My house. Just you and me," she says, giving me a smile.

"Sure. Stay where I can see you, beautiful," I say, then head back over to my spot by the door. Tonight is the night that I'll officially claim her ass again. This time I'm playing for keeps.

Chapter Twelve
Shane

I help Tiff into the house and close the door behind us. She decided to drink a little too much and was dancing on tables. I said enough was enough and left work early to make sure she got home safe.

Luke is at my mom's for the night and I plan on taking advantage of the situation. So long as she doesn't pass out.

"Are you ready to have some fun, sweetheart?" I ask her, and she wraps her arms around my neck, burying her body into mine.

"I'm not that drunk, handsome, and I want you," she purrs and rubs her body against mine. My dick is rock hard and ready to be let loose.

I take a step back and look at my beautiful woman, her green dress bunched up around her wide hips.

"Clothes off now!"

She grabs the bottom of the green sparkly dress she is wearing and slowly and seductively pulls it up over her head and drops it on the floor. Soon after, her bra and underwear join it on the floor.

"Is this what you wanted?" she breathlessly asks, her chest rising and falling quickly with each breath. Her eyes are dilated and filled with lust and yearning.

I pull off my shirt, my pants and boots following suit and landing on the floor next to me. I stride towards her and stop two inches in front of her. I run my finger from her ear down in between her breasts and hear her intake of breath. She's still so responsive to my touch.

"I want to climb inside your body and stay there," she whispers.

"I don't think that's possible," I say, grabbing the back of her head and pulling her closer to my body. I can feel her hot breath on my face from her parted lips, and I plunge my tongue into her mouth. Our tongues dance around each other's to the beat of our hearts. The air around us crackles as our souls become one again. I pull away only long enough to pick her up in my arms and place her on the couch.

Working my way along her body, I circle her navel with my tongue before continuing down. When my breath touches her thigh, a tremor of desire causes her body to shake. I continue my onslaught and I swipe my tongue through her folds. Her legs start to shake and I take two of my fingers and enter her pussy, causing her to moan and her ass to lift up off the bed. I take both my arms and lower her back down and apply pressure so that I'm holding her in place. A few more strokes and I bite down on her clit. Her first orgasm of the night hits her hard. She screams out, her breathing labored.

"Shane, please make love to me!"

I make my way back up her body and hover over her, looking into her chocolate brown eyes. The love and desire I see in them has me going weak. I take my engorged shaft into my hand, entering her and not stopping until I'm in up to the hilt. I stay unmoving for a couple minutes, to keep from coming. She's fucking tight and I'm already wanting to release my load into her. Once I know I can continue, I slowly pull out and plunge back in, causing her to moan.

"Fuck, baby!"

I pick up my pace, fucking her hard and rough. I can feel her pussy pulsing and her walls clamp down, causing stars to appear in my vision. My balls tighten and I know that I'm close to coming. I keep up the assault on her pussy, hitting the spot that will have her coming and screaming out my name.

"Shane, I'm close!" she says through her panting. I drive into her three more times and her walls clamp down, causing her back to arch up off the bed.

"Shane!" she screams out.

"Tiffany!" I growl, coming deep inside of her. My arms give way and my body lands on top of hers. We both lay quietly until our breathing and our heartbeats return to normal.

I roll to my side, bringing her with me, kissing her with untamed joy and pouring all the love I have for her into it. She pulls away, looking into my eyes. She smiles, knowing that what she feels is showing in them.

"I love you, Shane."

I bring my hand up and swipe away the tear rolling down her cheek. She's mine and this time, I'm not letting her go.

"I love you, beautiful."

She lays her head on my chest once I'm laying flay on my back, and I wrap my arms around her, holding her tight against my body. I hear soft snoring and look down, seeing that she has fallen asleep. I lay here, thinking about what's to come, and eventually my eyes drift closed and all I see is darkness.

Chapter Thirteen
Tiffany

My eyes flutter open and I lay here for a minute so I can adjust to the light. My head is pounding and I feel like I'm going to puke. I know I drank a lot last night and I am now regretting it.

"Good morning, sweetheart," I hear, and I look up to see Shane looking down at me. I remember everything about last night and my pussy clenches. It was amazing and I want to do it again.

"Good morning," I say back and stretch, trying to get the kinks out of my body. This couch is not comfortable to sleep on.

"Go take a shower and get ready. We have to go get our son," he says, and I moan. I don't want to do anything today.

"Can't he stay a little longer? I'm enjoying just having time for ourselves."

"I have something planned for today," he says.

I remove myself slowly from his body and stand up. The way he looks at my naked body has a blush spreading over my body.

"Are you sure you don't want this?" I ask and run my finger through my folds and moan. I'm still sensitive down there.

"Not enough time. Go take your shower, baby," he says, and I turn around, stomping into my room. I will get him to make love to me again. It's only a matter of time.

I turn the water to hot and hop in, grabbing the shampoo and washing my hair. Then I grab my body wash and clean my body. Once I'm done, I step out and dry off before heading into my bedroom to get dressed. I exit my bedroom and head into the living room. I see that Shane is fully dressed and ready to go.

"Ready, beautiful?"

"Yes," I answer, and we exit the house. I lock the door before heading over to his truck. He helps me in before heading over to his side, then he starts the truck and pulls off.

"Where are we going after picking him up?" I ask, looking over at him.

"It's a surprise," is all he says, so I look back out at the passing scenery. Our little town is beautiful with all the small stores and left-over St. Patrick's decorations up. It's like one of those towns in the Hallmark Christmas movies.

We pull up to his mom's house and he exits the truck and heads up to the door. A couple minutes later, he is heading back to the truck with a very excited Luke.

"Mommy! Daddy says we going somewhere!" he yells out.

"Yes, but he won't tell me where."

"I know," he says and smiles. I love that he is so happy.

"You told him, but not me," I say, scoffing.

"It's your surprise," he says, smiling. I love this man so much, it hurts. He's so sweet and loving.

He pulls off and we head out. He's taking the back roads, and all I see is fields and nothing more. An hour later we pull up at this quaint little restaurant a couple towns over. It's a small bed and breakfast like the ones in movies I have watched.

"Come on," he says and gets out, then helps our son out. I get out and meet them in front of the truck, then we head inside. It's beautiful and I don't want to leave. A woman with graying hair, green eyes, and a beautiful, wide smile greets us as we walk in.

"You must be Shane," she says and he nods, smiling.

"We have the space reserved for you," she says and ushers us into a small dining room. There is a table that has flowers in the middle of it and place settings in three spots. It's very romantic and sweet.

"Thank you, Sheryl," he says, and we all take our seats.

"How did you know about this place?"

"My mother. She and my dad came here all the time for their anniversaries."

"That's so sweet," I say and look down at the little menu in front of me.

Sheryl comes back out and I order the two-egg breakfast with toast, bacon, hash browns, and coffee. Then my two men order their meals.

"What's the occasion?" I ask, my eyebrow lifting. No one comes to a place like this without having a motive behind it.

"Let's eat then we will get to the surprise," he says with a smirk on his face.

"Mommy is going to love it!" Luke screams out, wiggling in his chair.

"Shh...don't give it away, buddy," Shane says, and Luke giggles. I love seeing them like this.

Our food arrives and we all dig in, eating in comfortable silence. Every two seconds I'm stealing looks at the man I have loved since high school. A man who has grown to be strong and courageous. He's always been the take charge kind of of man, but now he's hardened from being in the military and a lot more alpha when it comes to sex.

"Okay. I think you've waited long enough," Shane says and pulls a black box out of his pocket. Is he doing what I think he's doing?

"Tiffany, I made mistakes with you before I left. I have loved you for a long time and never stopped. You have given me a son and hopefully more in the future. You are it for me. Will you marry me?"

Oh my God! I've been waiting for this for a long time. Tears are running down my face and I know so is snot. This is the man I want for the rest of my life.

"Yes, I'll marry you!" I exclaim, and he takes the ring and slips it onto my finger. I pull my hand back and look at it. It's a small diamond surrounded by small rubies, and the band is a white gold. It's absolutely gorgeous.

"Yay!" I hear Luke yell, and I smile. This is the first day of the rest of our lives and I plan on making them happy ones.

Epilogue
Shane

Three months later...

We are heading to the park so our son can get some energy out after Tiffany's doctor's appointment this morning. Three weeks after I proposed, she found out she was pregnant. To say I'm excited is an understatement. We are having another baby and I'm happy.

"When are you going to tell me?" I ask for the hundredth time.

"At the right time, my sexy man," she says, and I smile.

"Fine!" I growl. I pull into the park and shut off the truck.

"Come on, Daddy!" my son yells, and I get out and help him out. He runs over to the swing set and stands there waiting for us. I help my pregnant and beautiful woman out, then we head towards where Luke is standing.

"Daddy, will you push me?" he asks, and I pick him up and settle him in the baby swing. He's still not ready for the big kids one yet. He squeals and swings his legs, almost catching me in the face.

"It's so peaceful here," Tiff says and sits down on the bench next to the swing set. She rubs her stomach and looks back up at me, a gorgeous smile on her face.

"How are you feeling?" I ask and push my son a little higher. I hear him giggle. He swings out with his legs again and I duck out of the way. This kid is trying to hurt me.

"I'm fine. We're having a baby girl," she says, and right at that moment the swing comes back towards me and his feet catch me in the groin area. I drop to the ground holding my dick in my hand and hear Luke and Tiff laughing at my pain. She distracted me on purpose and she will pay for it.

"Are you alright down there?" I hear, and I look up at my woman. She has a smile on her face and a twinkle of mischief in her eyes.

"I'm fine," I growl and stand up, taking her into my arms. This is one of the happiest days of my life. I'm getting a daughter.

"I love you," I tell her, and plant a chaste kiss on her lips. She moans and settles her body closer to mine. Sex has been awesome between us and I love hearing her moans and screams.

"I love you," she says, and I kiss her again. This time it's not as sweet. This is how I want us to be until the day we both pass away. I also plan on having at least two more children, but that's for another time. I got lucky that she gave me a second chance. All my family will know that I love them and that I'll support them in every way.

Be Sure To Check Out The Rest Of The Lucky In Love Series

M.K. Moore Forever Lucky
Luckiest Love by Rachelle Stevensen LINK COMING SOON!
S.E. Isaac Just My Luck
S.A. Clayton Lucky Charm
April Lynn Baker Luck and Love
ChaShiree M. Lucky Timing
Alana Winters Lucky Star
Falling for Lucky by Andi Lynn LINK COMING SOON!
Euryia Larsen Clover's Luck
Luck of the Draw by Lia Violet LINK COMING SOON!
AvaPearl Luck of the Lass
Imani Jay Stroke of Luck
W A Marlow For Luck's Sake
Lucky You by V. Kelly LINK COMING SOON!
Lucky Girl by KL Fast & M.K. Moore LINK COMING SOON!

About the Author

I am a Bestselling and International Bestselling Author from Franklin, IN and enjoys spending time with family and friends. I got my love of romance from Danielle Steel, Nora Roberts and the Twilight Series. I love writing about Alphas who are dominant but love their women. I also go under the penname of J.D. Amore for PNR.

Follow April Lynn Baker

www.ingramcontent.com/pod-product-compliance
Lightning Source LLC
Chambersburg PA
CBHW051404150726
48000CB00003B/1327